FOXTROT

START

CHA CHA

START

& LOLA

RHUMBA

WALTZ

STERLING and the distinctive Sterling logo are registered trademarks of
Sterling Publishing Co., Inc.

10 9 8 7 6 5 4 3 2 1

Published by Sterling Publishing Co., Inc.
387 Park Avenue South, New York, NY 10016
Text © 2009 by Tammi Sauer
Illustrations © 2009 by Dan Santat
Distributed in the United Kingdom by GMC Distribution Services
Castle Place, 166 High Street, Lewes, East Sussex, England BN7 1XU

The illustrations in this book were created using
acrylic and ink with Adobe PhotoShop

ISBN 978-1-4027-8083-7

Designed by Kate Moll and Dan Santat

CHICKEN DANCE

written by **TAMMI SAUER**

illustrated by **DAN SANTAT**

STERLING

New York / London

FOR MY MOM, RAMONA KIPPES, WHO TOTALLY BAWKS AND ROLLS. - T.S.

FOR LEAH, ALEK, AND KYLE. - D.S.

Marge and Lola took one look at the poster on the barn door and almost lost their cluck. Elvis Poultry was *top bird.* They had to win those tickets.

The ducks paraded by.
"Don't bother, drumsticks."
"Ducks win every year."
"All a chicken can do is bawk, flap, and shake."
Marge and Lola ignored the quackers and tested
out their talents.

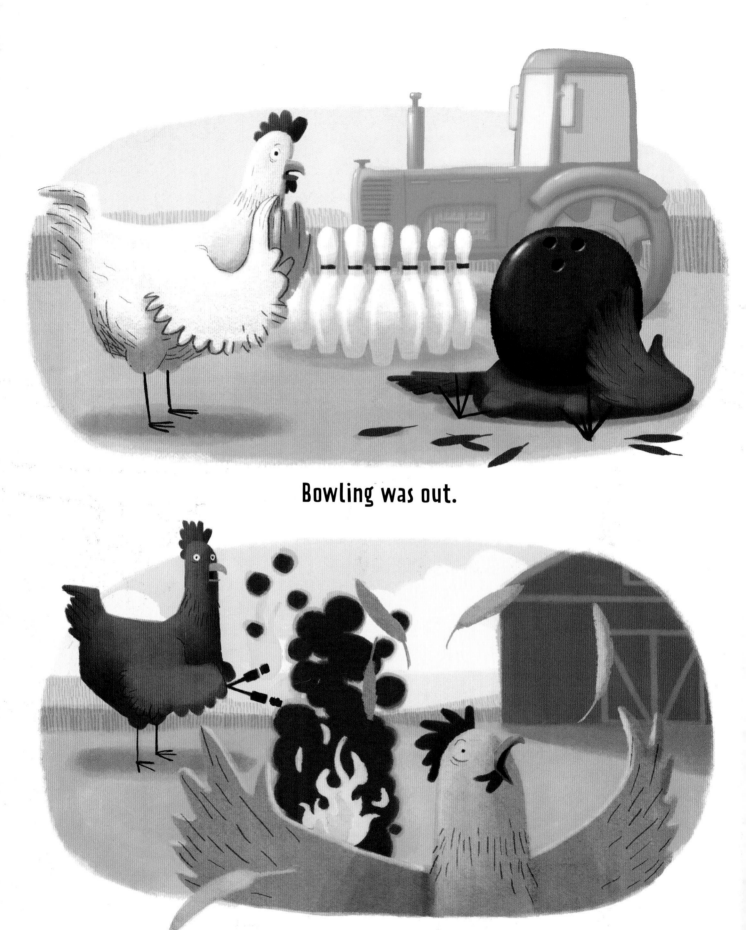

Bowling was out.

So was juggling.

And tightrope walking.

"We could try flying," Marge said.
Lola grinned. "Flying chickens?
Now that's talent!"
The chickens scrambled to the top
of the coop.

They sank in hay up to their wattles.
The ducks flew by.
"Bail out, chickens!" they called down below.

Marge and Lola dusted themselves off and shook hay
from their feathers.
"Now what?" asked Lola.
"We could try swimming," said Marge.
Lola nodded. "Swimming chickens? Now that's talent!"

The chickens tottered
to the pond.

They
jumped.

They
fluttered.

They totally sank.

The ducks swam by.
"Get some floaties, chickens!"

Marge and Lola waded ashore and spit water from their beaks.
"Any other big ideas?" said Lola.
Marge stared at the setting sun. "Too late. It's show time.
We'll have to wing it."
The chickens bumbled to the barn, found their seats, and
settled in for the show.

The goats ate a tractor and scored a seven.
"Not bad," said Marge.

The pigs formed a pyramid and scored an eight.

"I've seen better," said Lola.

The cows jumped over the moon.

"That's old!" said Lola. "We can still win this thing!"
Suddenly, trumpets sounded.

The crowd gasped.
The ducks grabbed their boards and hit the water.

They scored . . .

. . . a nine.
The barnyard went wild.

Smirking at the chickens, the ducks flounced back to their seats.
"We're on," said Marge.
"We're doomed," said Lola.
The chickens shuffled onstage.
They blinked at the crowd.
And gulped.

"What's the matter?" yelled a duck.

"Are you chicken?"

This put the chickens in a foul mood.

They BAWKED. They FLAPPED. They SHOOK.

"More! More! More!"
the crowd chanted.

Marge and Lola looked at each other.
"But we're just doing regular chicken stuff," Marge whispered.
"Regular chicken stuff? Now *that's* talent!" Lola grabbed a mike.
"Let's bawk and roll!"

The chickens **BAWKED** and **FLAPPED** and **SHOOK** all over the stage.

They scored . . .

. . . an eight-point five.

"Losers!" the ducks called as they plucked the tickets from the prize table. "Ducks rule."

Marge and Lola gazed at the tickets and wiped their eyes.
Then, from the top of the barn, a voice crooned—
"You chicks rocked!"
A rooster swooped to the stage. "You had me all shook up."

Elvis Poultry was in the building.

Elvis smoothed his crest. "I could use an act like yours."
Before Marge and Lola could say a word, duck feathers flew.
The ducks lunged at the chickens when—

THUNK!

THUNK!

—the cows came home, scoring a perfect ten.

The next day, a new poster was tacked
on every barn in the countryside . . .

DISCO CHICKEN

START

GRAPEVINE

GRAPEVINE LEFT

GRAPEVINE RIGHT

START

CHATTANOOGA CHOO CHOO

CROSS KICK